Ross

Pencilympics

A Pencilmation Story

by Jake Black
illustrated by JJ Harrison

PENGUIN YOUNG READERS LICENSES
AN IMPRINT OF PENGUIN RANDOM HOUSE LLC, NEW YORK

FIRST PUBLISHED IN THE UNITED STATES OF AMERICA
BY PENGUIN YOUNG READERS LICENSES, AN IMPRINT OF
PENGUIN RANDOM HOUSE LLC, NEW YORK, 2023

VISIT US ONLINE AT PENGUINRANDOMHOUSE.COM.

MANUFACTURED IN CHINA

ISBN 9780593659090 10 9 8 7 6 5 4 3 2 1 TOPL

DESIGN BY TAYLOR ABATIELL

CHAPTER ONE

It was a beautiful, sunny day, and Pencilmate was enjoying the warm air as he strolled through the park. Whistling to himself, he saw kids roller-skating, a woman chasing a butterfly with a net, and a family buying ice-cream cones from a stand.

It was the perfect day. His thoughts immediately turned to what sort of mischief he could conjure up.

As he scanned the area, there wasn't anything too tempting at the moment. But he was sure he'd figure something out. Mischief was, after all, what he was best at. As he continued his walk, something caught his eye: a series of signs hanging on a fence at the far side of the park. They were illustrated in bright, colorful pictures, and though he couldn't read them from this distance, Pencilmate had to know what they said.

Scurrying across the park toward the signs, Pencilmate leaped over a girl drawing in sidewalk chalk, somersaulted around an elderly couple sitting on a park bench, and dove behind a group of teenagers playing ultimate Frisbee. Soon, he reached his destination. His eyes grew wide as he gazed at the massive series of signs.

"Coming soon! The Pencilympics!" read the first sign. The rest were a sequence of posters advertising the events of the exciting athletic competition. Basketball! Karate! Thumb wrestling! Skateboarding! And the final event was a triathlon—swimming, biking, and running!

Pencilmate rubbed his chin as he read the different events. He felt his excitement grow within him. He knew he could do most of those sports, and the ones he hadn't learned before, he would be able to master quickly. He closed his eyes and imagined himself competing in each event.

In his mind, Pencilmate saw himself scoring a game-winning three-pointer in the basketball game, breaking a stack of boards with a karate chop, dominating an opponent in a thumb-wrestling contest, flipping a wild trick on his skateboard, and crossing the finish line in the triathlon. The first step to victory, Pencilmate knew, was to envision it.

Only one challenge remained: figuring out how to sign up for the Pencilympics.

Just then, Pencilmate heard a voice speaking over a staticky loudspeaker elsewhere in the park.

"HEAR YE, HEAR YE! Don't miss your chan‹sktch› to compete with the grea‹sktch›est athletes in our wor‹sktch› in the Pencilympics! Sign-ups begin today here in the p‹sktch›! Don't miss your chance to win the quadrillion doll‹sktch› prize!" the voice said through static.

Pencilmate's eyes widened.

"A quadrillion dollars?!" he said to himself. "That's more money than I'll ever see in about ten lifetimes! I *have* to win this competition."

His eyes suddenly fixed themselves on the man speaking into the loudspeaker at a far corner of the park. He was standing on a large podium next to a table with a sign reading "Pencilympics Sign-Ups." A line was already beginning to form.

Pencilmate sprinted across the park. Before he could really build up speed, the tip of his shoe fell into a crack in the sidewalk. He rolled head over heels about five times before stopping on a patch of grass. Standing back up, he saw the Pencilympics sign-up line continuing to grow. *I have to get there fast!* he thought.

Suddenly, he saw a boy on a scooter coming up behind him. That would work!

To his left, Pencilmate saw a group of girls playing hopscotch. He casually walked over to their game and, hoping they wouldn't notice, picked up their hopscotch pebble. With a flick of his sure-to-be-thumb-wrestling-champion thumb, he tossed the pebble directly in front of the scooter's path.

The rider didn't see the pebble until it was too late. The front wheel of his scooter ran into the pebble like it was a massive speed bump, sending the scooter and rider soaring through the air. As the boy landed on a pile of leaves, his scooter crashed directly in front of Pencilmate. Pencilmate lifted the scooter and rapidly rode his way toward the line.

The journey to the Pencilympics line was without further incident. Pencilmate reached the back of the very long line and tossed the scooter away. Standing at the back of the line, he quickly grew impatient. "This will take forever! If all these people sign up, my chances of winning that quadrillion-dollar prize are gone!" he said. He had to act fast!

Looking around, he noticed a piece of cloth nearby, blowing in the breeze. Wrapping that cloth around a fallen tree limb he found on the ground, Pencilmate pretended it was a fussing baby. "Awww there, there!" he cooed.

As he made crying sounds, several kindhearted people allowed Pencilmate and his "baby" to move ahead of them in line. He was getting closer, but not close enough.

A new scheme popped into his head. Tossing the fake baby away, Pencilmate got down on the ground and slithered his way like a snake around and through the feet and legs of several more people ahead of him in line. Having cut in front of more than a dozen waiting potential Pencilympians, he popped up, standing in the line as though he'd been there the entire time. Still, there was a ways to go before he would reach the registration table.

Growing more impatient, Pencilmate came up with another scheme to get ahead in the line even faster. Using a broken clipboard he spotted in a nearby garbage can, he posed as a Pencilympics official, asking a series of questions to each of the competitors ahead of him in line. This was a very effective plan until one of the other athletes noticed Pencilmate didn't have any paper on his clipboard. Throwing away the clipboard, he raced ahead a few more people and slid into the line, hiding his face from the others to prevent being discovered.

From his new place in line, Pencilmate surveyed his surroundings. This was a time for desperate action. Without thinking, he scurried up the back of the person in front of him and, with great flair, run-jumped from the shoulders and heads of several people. It was a display of pencil-parkour unlike any the world had ever seen. Within seconds, he reached the head of the line. Only he was moving so swiftly across the top of the queue that he didn't notice it was time to stop running. He leaped ahead as though there were another person in the line in front of him.

He soared through the air, arms and legs flailing as he flew. In a matter of seconds that felt like hours, Pencilmate descended from his lofty heights, crashing into the registration table and causing it to explode into shards and slivers. Undaunted, he stood up and filled out the registration paperwork to compete for the quadrillion-dollar Pencilympics prize.

After he signed his name at the bottom of the form and left it on the broken table, he turned back to see everyone he'd encountered along his way furiously looking at him. The hopscotch girls were growling, the scooter boy gritted his teeth, and the rest of the line seemed as though they were ready to tear him limb from limb.

Pencilmate grinned and dashed away before the angry mob could catch him and exact their revenge. Glad to escape, Pencilmate laughed as he ran. There was a lot of training Pencilmate had to do if he was going to win the prestigious competition and unimaginable prize!

CHAPTER TWO

The Pencilympics were only a few days away, and Pencilmate knew that if he wanted to win the quadrillion-dollar prize, he would have to train like he'd never trained before!

He ventured out into town to find a gym he could work out in. It had to have a lot of different equipment for him to get game ready! Soon, he found a gym filled with the latest exercise machines. It was like an athletic wonderland!

Regaining his focus, Pencilmate started blasting a playlist of his favorite hair metal workout music from his portable music player. With an elastic headband around his head, a towel around his neck, and his athletic shoes on, Pencilmate set out to exercise.

He decided to start with some rigorous cardio. Pencilmate stepped onto a treadmill. It began slowly at first: walking speed, really. *This is nothing! I know I can do more than this,* he thought. *Let's speed things up!*

Pencilmate increased the speed slightly and started to jog. Still manageable, though a bit more strenuous than the starting pace had been. Beads of sweat trickled down his face. He smiled, feeling the burn. That quadrillion-dollar prize was sure to be his!

He upped the speed a touch more. This was getting a little harder. *But, after all, no pain, no gain!* Pencilmate thought. He was able to keep time with the increasing speed and wanted to challenge himself a bit more. He reached for the button to up his velocity a little but accidentally hit the button marked "FULL SPEED."

The treadmill instantly accelerated. Pencilmate felt his legs spinning beneath him. The treadmill was moving so quickly and Pencilmate was running so frantically that his towel and headband flew off! It was almost like his shoes couldn't even touch the treadmill. He was doing it! He was keeping up with the machine's speed!

Within a few seconds, however, all was lost. He paused for less than a second, and the treadmill grabbed his shoes and pulled Pencilmate around the running loop, under the machine, and inside its gears before spitting him out, sending him flying across the room and crashing into a wall.

"I think that's enough running for today," Pencilmate panted.

He scanned the gym and saw a large barbell just begging to be lifted. Standing over the large weight, he rubbed his hands together, curled his fingers around the center bar that connected the two massive spherical dumbbells, and hoisted it upward with all his might. To his great surprise, the bar went straight up, leaving the dumbbells on the ground!

That won't help. Determined to lift the dumbbells, Pencilmate drove the bar into the top of one of the spherical weights, so that it stuck upright. With renewed, intense effort, he picked up the other dumbbell.

Grunting, panting, sweating, and straining, Pencilmate lifted the giant lead ball up and placed it atop the bar. Proud of his successful effort, he looked at the repaired barbell like a trophy. That was until the dumbbell he just placed atop the bar fell off, smashing his foot!

"Aaaahhhhh!!!" Pencilmate cried out in pain as he struggled to free his foot from underneath the weight. After getting his foot free, he faced another setback as the once upright bar fell, hitting him on the head.

Pencilmate felt his frustration growing within him. "I'll show that barbell who's boss!" he yelled.

Enraged, he put the barbell back together. His anger reached a fever pitch as he lifted the weights above his head. Holding the barbell above him, Pencilmate smiled at his achievement. That was until both dumbbells fell from the bar, landing on his feet!

After another painful cry, Pencilmate decided to move on from the dumbbells and over to a different form of training: boxing. In the middle of the gym, there was a large boxing ring surrounded by lights. Athletes could work on their technique by shadowboxing. They even had some jump ropes for the boxers to warm up with hanging on the ring ropes!

Pencilmate stepped through the ring ropes and into the fabled squared circle. He watched his shadow as he jabbed and uppercut his way through a routine. *Punching the air is a lot easier than lifting weights or running full speed on a treadmill,* he thought.

Suddenly, Pencilmate felt something strike

his midsection. He looked around but didn't see anyone else in the gym. He resumed his boxing practice and again felt something hit him.

"Oof!" Confused, Pencilmate tentatively started swinging at the air again. Soon enough he noticed his attacker.

It was his shadow! And it was ready to rumble!

Pencilmate was pummeled by his shadow, and though he tried very hard, he couldn't figure out how to strike back. His shadow danced around him, engaging in fisticuffs for several minutes.

Getting desperate, Pencilmate took off his shoe and threw it at his shadow. He missed his intended target but smashed one of the lights surrounding the ring! He noticed his shadow instantly got a little smaller.

"Aha!" Pencilmate said and threw his

other shoe at another light, shattering it and reducing the size of his adversary. Thinking fast, Pencilmate grabbed a jump rope that was hanging on the ropes and made it into a lasso. He wrangled the remaining lights around the ring, dragging them to the ground and destroying them.

As darkness encompassed the gym, Pencilmate laughed victoriously. "That's what I call a knockout!"

Having accomplished everything he wanted to do in his training at the gym, and because it was literally so dark he couldn't see anything, Pencilmate put his shoes back on and went outside to find a drink.

"Soooo thirsty . . . ," Pencilmate gasped.

The hot sun bore down on him and sweat poured out of him. He had never been hotter or thirstier. He dragged his exhausted, dehydrated body down the road. There was no water to be seen anywhere. He quickly grew so weary that he collapsed, certain that doom was set to befall him!

Within a matter of moments, however, a devilish being appeared in front of him. The monster teased Pencilmate with a cool, refreshing bottle of soda.

"You want it?" the monster asked, smiling evilly.

Nodding desperately, Pencilmate reached for it, but the monster snatched it away. With a snap of his fingers, he set up a chessboard between him and Pencilmate. Pencilmate understood. He had to defeat the monster in chess to win the desperately sought beverage.

The monster made several dominant moves to open the match. Undaunted, Pencilmate moved his queen across the board, capturing

several pieces and cornering the king all in one fell swoop.

"Checkmate!" he crowed. He snatched the soda from the demon and walked away, ready for his drink. But there was a small problem: He couldn't open the bottle! He struggled and struggled with the cap, but it just wouldn't budge.

The monster reappeared and demanded that Pencilmate read the rules of chess. "You cheated!" he yelled.

Pencilmate dismissed the demon's concerns but had an idea.

He motioned for the monster to open the soda bottle. Confused, the monster agreed. As he unscrewed the cap, the entire contents of the soda bottle sprayed him in the face. Pencilmate laughed. Then a surprising thing happened. The monster started to laugh. They both laughed, high-fived each other, and shared another soda that the demon made appear out of nowhere.

The two new friends parted ways, the monster returning to his underworld home and Pencilmate setting course back to his place. The Pencilympics were only a few days away, and he was determined to be ready when the first events began.

CHAPTER THREE

"Let the games begin!" the Pencilympics official announced.

Still desperately wanting the quadrillion-dollar prize, Pencilmate made sure he understood the competition's rules. He didn't have to win every event, just some of them. He needed to rack up enough points through winning, or coming close to winning, so that by the end of the games he'd be at the top of the mountain—the top of the mountain of money, that is!

And with that, Pencilmate was ready to put all his training to work. The first round was basketball. There was already a large crowd at the court waiting for the game to start.

Pencilmate wasn't modest enough to say he was bad at basketball. He believed he was great. And after today, everyone else would believe it, too.

Pencilmate tied his shoes and set out to the court for a rousing game of one-on-one. He grabbed the ball, immediately showing off his skills as a baller by doing tricky dribbling routines and spinning the ball on his index finger.

He threw the ball in a long-distance shot. ***SWISH!*** It went straight into the basket.

But Pencilmate didn't see it come through the net. Confused, he approached the goal. He looked up through the bottom of the hoop. No ball. He scaled the post, climbing over the backboard and staring down through the basket. Still no ball. He even dove into the basket, getting stuck inside for a moment, but still could not find the ball.

Suddenly, it was like his legs and body disappeared, and his head fell through the hoop, bouncing on the court like the ball.

Shaking the pain off his bouncing face, but for some reason still not able to find or feel his legs, Pencilmate looked up and saw his opponent dribbling the ball. The opponent's tricks were better than Pencilmate's. He was spinning the ball on his fingers and even his toes. But suddenly, the ball disappeared just like it had before.

The opponent glanced around the court, as confused as Pencilmate had been. Pencilmate's eyes grew wide when he realized he himself looked like a basketball. His opponent came to that same realization and picked up Pencilmate's head, spinning the disembodied Pencilmate on his fingers and toes before dribbling him across the court.

"Nonononononono!" Pencilmate cried out.

Laughing at Pencilmate's misery, his opponent dribbled down the court and lobbed up a long shot much like Pencilmate had moments before.

"Auuuggghhhhh!" Pencilmate screamed as he soared skyward. The shot was so high, Pencilmate was sure he could see clouds. And then he began his descent toward the basket.

"Auuuggghhhhh!" he screamed again as he flew closer and closer to the hoop.

His head landed with a thud on the basket. To Pencilmate's surprise, he didn't fall through the basket again. It seemed his head was too big to fit! He circled and circled the bucket. His opponent looked on in horror, literally falling to his knees in a prayer of desperation.

Pencilmate pursed his lips and let out a slight breath, propelling him off the basket and onto the court. As he landed, his opponent cried out in frustration and ran off. Pencilmate laughed victoriously. Meanwhile, his legs and body reappeared just as suddenly as they'd disappeared moments before.

He stood up ready for the next basketball challenge. A new opponent took to the court, dribbling the ball. This new opponent was an even better player than the last. He dribbled his way around Pencilmate to score the first points of the game. Pencilmate responded with some quick points of his own.

Pencilmate and his opponent both worked hard, scoring lots of points and staying neck and neck throughout the fast-paced game.

The evenly matched contest came down to the final shot. Pencilmate's new opponent threw it up from a long distance and sank it to score the win!

Devastated, Pencilmate dropped to the floor. A crowd had gathered around his opponent with everyone high-fiving each other.

Thinking it might help him feel better, Pencilmate wanted in on that action and scurried over to the cheering crowd, his hand raised for a high five. He approached the cheering throngs but was left hanging. No one high-fived him or even noticed he was there. He ran over to the referee, who ignored him. Even the court custodian ignored him.

Frustrated, Pencilmate parked himself on the bench at the sidelines, his hand still up for a high five. Soon, he was covered in the shadow of his conquering opponent. Pencilmate looked up at the towering victor. The opponent also had his hand raised, poised for a high five.

Confused, Pencilmate pointed to himself, asking if the opponent wanted to high-five him. The opponent simply nodded.

Pencilmate's smile twisted itself into a nefarious grin. Now was his chance for vengeance on the rival who had vanquished him. He leaped from his seat on the bench, soaring toward the opponent. The opponent likewise launched himself skyward. The two competitors flew toward one another, their hands raised and ready to smack each other in the ultimate show of sportsmanship.

As they drew close, Pencilmate snidely withdrew his hand, causing his opponent's hand to miss. The opponent crashed on the court face-first. Pencilmate couldn't help but laugh. And laugh. And laugh.

His angry opponent pulled himself up from the court, glaring at Pencilmate. Not content with simply laughing at his opponent's humiliation, Pencilmate danced an ornate victory dance. The opponent, the referee, the crowd, and even the court custodian grew angry at Pencilmate's display of poor sportsmanship. However, Pencilmate, who continued dancing his celebratory routine, was oblivious to them.

The group gathered around Pencilmate, everyone raising their hands for high fives. Pencilmate saw the gathering group, his excitement growing for all the high fives he was about to receive. He mirrored their actions, raising his arms to slap palms with as many people as possible. However, his glee turned to terror as he noticed everyone in the mob had curled their fingers, closing their open palms into fists. In a flash, they let Pencilmate know how they felt about his display. Collectively, the angry mob catapulted Pencilmate across the court and directly into the basket, where he landed headfirst.

The mob cheered as they departed the court, leaving Pencilmate stuck in the hoop. Hours passed and the arena grew dark. Nevertheless, Pencilmate, relieved that his legs hadn't disappeared again, couldn't stop smiling. He may not have won the first round of the basketball game, but he got the last laugh on his opponents. And, even in losing, he scored enough points in the competition that he was still on his way to the quadrillion-dollar prize. He was certain he would win the next round and the round after that, and the round after that, until the prize was his.

That is, if he could ever get down from the basketball hoop.

CHAPTER FOUR

Having accumulated enough points to believe he would advance in (and win!) the Pencilympics, Pencilmate prepared for the next competition: a karate tournament.

"I better practice," Pencilmate said.

He flailed his arms and legs around in a haphazard fashion, while yelling out, "Hi-yaaaaa!"

He quickly came to a disturbing realization.

"I don't know karate!" he cried out in a panic.

Remembering his goal for the quadrillion-dollar prize, Pencilmate set out into town, searching for someone who could train him in the ways of the ancient martial arts. Soon, he discovered Koko's Karate School, a majestic- and mysterious-looking building. There, Pencilmate knew, he would unlock the physical and mental powers of karate he needed to score the prize money.

However, he encountered his first obstacle at the dojo's front door. Pencilmate tried pushing on the door with no success. He then pulled on the door but was still unable to open it. Confused and a little frustrated, Pencilmate leaned his back on the door, causing it to slide sideways. The door now open, he finally had access to the school.

The minimalistic decorations within the dojo drew Pencilmate's eyes to the center of the room. There sat Koko, his eyes closed, deep in meditation.

"I know why you have come," Koko said.

Pencilmate opened his mouth to respond, but

before he could say anything, Koko cut him off. "You have a desire to learn the great secrets of the karate masters."

Koko sprang to his feet and bowed toward Pencilmate. Pencilmate returned the bow, a little nervous.

"Karate brings focus to one's mind and peace to one's heart. Your intentions must be pure if you are to master the centuries-old martial arts," Koko said softly.

Pencilmate's face contorted in a look of frustrated impatience. "I need to be a black belt by tomorrow," he said.

Koko looked horrified. "Impossible!"

The karate master struck what appeared to be an attack stance. Frightened, Pencilmate stepped backward. Koko raised his hands and conjured a black belt out of thin air. He held it toward Pencilmate, who reached out for it.

Koko snapped it back, pulling away from him.

"This is what you seek, but you must learn to control your emotions before you learn the art of karate," Koko said.

The martial arts master tossed the black belt away and motioned for Pencilmate to sit on the floor. He descended to the ground and resumed his meditation. Pencilmate sat and tried imitating what he saw Koko doing. He closed his eyes and drew in a deep breath, causing him to cough violently. He settled himself back in position, noticing Koko was undisturbed.

He continued his attempts to meditate. *But this is so boooooorrriiiiingggg,* he thought. He opened one eye and peeked at his surroundings. He noticed the black belt still resting on the floor.

Pencilmate tiptoed around Koko to retrieve the belt.

However, before he could reach it, the karate

instructor leaped to his feet, landing in between Pencilmate and the belt. In a flurry of moves, Koko struck Pencilmate and seemed to make the belt disappear.

"Uggghhhh," Pencilmate groaned as he pulled himself off the ground.

"Now, you are ready," Koko whispered.

Koko snapped his fingers and a stack of bricks atop two wooden beams appeared. With great ease, Koko smashed the bricks in a swift karate chop.

Koko snapped his fingers again and another stack of bricks appeared in front of Pencilmate. Koko motioned for Pencilmate to destroy them as he had. Confident, Pencilmate smirked. He puffed out his chest, took in a deep breath, popped his knuckles, and reared back, ready to deliver a mighty chop to the bricks.

He threw his hand forward in a powerful chop that collided with the bricks. The stack didn't budge, but Pencilmate was sure he heard a cracking sound in his hand on its impact with the bricks.

"Aaaauuuuggghhhhhh!" Pencilmate cried out in agony.

Koko, embarrassed on Pencilmate's behalf, made all but one of the bricks disappear from the stack. Pencilmate balled up his hand, determined to break this last brick. He slammed his fist into it with such force that when it, too, didn't break, Pencilmate felt as though he had shattered into a fine powder.

Koko transformed the brick into a twig for his student. Pencilmate laughed nervously as he approached the thin piece of wood. He slammed his hand on the twig. It didn't break! He repeatedly chopped at the twig, but no matter how hard he hit it, he couldn't get it to break.

Koko calmly and quietly made the twig disappear before motioning for Pencilmate to leave. "I have no more to teach you," he said.

Devastated, Pencilmate watched his sensei leave the room for the back of the dojo. His disappointment turned to excitement, however, as he came up with a devilish idea.

Pencilmate followed Koko into the back room, where he saw his teacher drinking some tea. He snuck up behind him, snatching Koko's black belt from around his waist. Pencilmate escaped before Koko even noticed his missing belt. However, when he stood up from his table, his gi fell to the floor, exposing his pink-heart bedazzled underwear!

The following day, Pencilmate stood across the mat from his opponent in the Pencilympics karate competition, dressed in a gi of his own with Koko's black belt around his waist. The crowd cheered as the two competitors prepared for the match. Each was posed in a strong stance, hoping to intimidate the other. The referee called for the fight to begin, but before either athlete could strike the other, Pencilmate felt someone tap on his shoulder. He turned around to see Koko still clad in his underwear.

"You have something that belongs to me," Koko said, launching into a whirlwind of strikes and kicks.

The crowd gasped in unison as they watched Koko take back his black belt.

As the dust settled around Pencilmate, Koko pulled out the twig, motioning for Pencilmate to break it. Bruised, battered, and embarrassed, Pencilmate looked to take out his rage on the twig. He threw the fastest, strongest, most vicious chop he could muster.

Once again, it did not break. Frustrated and embarrassed, Pencilmate kicked the twig. It bent but did not break. He snatched it from Koko's hands and tried breaking it over his knee. But it did not break. He banged it on the ground. Still nothing!

Furious, Pencilmate threw the twig across the mat. His opponent, an actual black belt in karate, picked up the twig. Smiling, his eyes fixed on Pencilmate, the opponent tossed the twig into the air.

REF

Yelling "Kiii-yyyyyy," the opponent chopped and kicked at the twig, slicing it into a dozen separate pieces that fell to the mat in the shape of a yin-yang symbol.

Koko laughed loudly at his former student's misfortune. He was soon joined by the crowd, whose laughter only added to Pencilmate's frustration. Pencilmate felt his face grow red with humiliation. However, that apparent embarrassment passed quickly as the karate competition's judges made a startling announcement. Because Koko attacked Pencilmate just as the competition was to begin, Pencilmate's opponent automatically forfeited the match, making Pencilmate the winner!

The karate event's points were added to his Pencilympics score, putting him high on the list of finalists with only three events to go!

Pencilmate danced an ornate victory dance in front of his opponent and Koko, who could only stare at their vanquisher in stunned silence.

CHAPTER FIVE

With only three contests to go, Pencilmate had to focus. He was in a good position as far as his accumulated points were concerned, but he wanted to have more of a cushion before he reached the finals. Fortunately, the next contest was something he'd been passionate about for all of his existence: thumb wrestling. He followed all the greats in the sport. He'd read all the magazines. Bought every pay-per-view event. Even sat ringside for some of the greatest thumb-wrestling battles of all time. His favorite thumb wrestler was the current reigning, defending thumb-wrestling heavyweight champion of the world, Russel.

Pencilmate gazed at a poster of Russel on his wall in admiration. For years, people made fun of Pencilmate for loving thumb wrestling. They repeatedly told him it was fake. But Pencilmate didn't care. To him it was the coolest sport in the world. And the fact that he would actually be competing in a thumb-wrestling ring as part of the Pencilympics thrilled him.

"I better train harder than I ever have," Pencilmate said. "Gotta follow Russel's four thumb-damentals: stretch, flex, build, and hydrate."

So that's just what he did. Pencilmate began a rigorous routine of stretching his thumb up and down, flexing his thumb muscles, and building indomitable strength in his digit. Over the course of several days, he could feel his thumb getting stronger. He attached small metal spheres with string and used his thumb to hoist them up as weights. And he was sure to hydrate. He didn't totally understand why Russel thought it was so important, but if you want to be the best, you have to follow the best's advice.

His thumb was ready. He gave a thumbs-up to the poster of Russel on his wall and headed for the tournament at the Pencilympics Arena. He was prepared to prove his dominance in this stage of the competition, his mind firmly fixed on the grand prize.

As had been the case throughout the Pencilympics, the arena was full of fans excited to watch the world-class competition. Pencilmate spied his parents cheering and waving to him high up in the stands. Slightly embarrassed, Pencilmate waved back but quickly refocused his attention on the task at hand . . . er . . . thumb.

His first match was against his little brother, Mini-Mate, whom Pencilmate had encountered a few times before and loathed. Mini-Mate looked just like Pencilmate, only smaller. Pencilmate stared down his rival doppelgänger with an intense fury.

"You're going down," Pencilmate whispered.

"Nah" was all Mini-Mate replied.

The bell rang, signaling the start of the match. The two opponents clasped their hands. Pencilmate's training immediately paid off as he made quick work of Mini-Mate, pinning the smaller person's thumb in a matter of seconds.

The crowd roared their approval! Mini-Mate slunk away, humiliated in defeat, as Pencilmate gave the audience a big thumbs-up. His parents cheered loudly.

The next opponent entered the ring: Tall Guy. Tall Guy literally towered over Pencilmate. He stroked his bushy mustache before extending his hand to Pencilmate.

"May the best man win," Tall Guy said.

"That'll be me," Pencilmate said, his eyes narrowing into a sharp focus on his opponent. Again, the bell rang, and the two contenders engaged in a vicious contest of thumbs. Just as before, however, Pencilmate made quick work of his opponent. He felt his thumb getting stronger with each victory.

He again raised a thumb to his adoring fans. This time, though, his thumb extended two little arms that flexed their muscles, posing for the crowd. Pencilmate stared at his suddenly ripped and autonomous thumb and smiled. He high-fived the thumb's tiny hand and prepared himself for his next opponent.

Granny, an elderly woman, stepped into the squared circle. Pencilmate laughed. Did she really think she stood a chance?! Granny glared back at him. She licked her thumb, Pencilmate's thumbs flexed their muscles, and the two combatants locked hands.

Pencilmate thought this would be an easy win, but it was a lot harder than he'd expected! Granny's thumb was smaller and faster, able to slip out of Pencilmate's attempts to pin or even wrestle. And though it took more work than the previous two opponents, Pencilmate eked out a win over the geriatric gladiator, pinning her frail thumb for the three count.

Pencilmate could taste victory. There was apparently only one opponent left standing in his way of claiming victory in the thumb-wrestling tournament and padding his score going into the final two events of the Pencilympics.

Suddenly, the crowd cheered louder and longer than they had before. Pencilmate waved to his fans, certain their cheers were for him. That was until he looked toward the entrance ramp that led to the ring. Pencilmate's face fell, and his heart sank into his stomach. His final opponent was the one thumb wrestler who'd long inspired him: the world champion, Russel.

Russel strode to the ring clad in an ornately bedazzled robe, the world championship belt attached firmly around his waist. Nervous sweat poured from Pencilmate. He looked down at his thumb who replied with a nervous shrug.

The referee called the two warriors to the center of the ring. Russel confidently stared down at Pencilmate. All of Pencilmate's confidence withered away.

The bell rang, and they clasped hands. Russel's championship experience was immediately evident. He drove his thumb down on Pencilmate's, folding it on itself like an accordion. Using all his might, Pencilmate pulled his thumb out from under Russel's before the count of three and charged toward his opponent's digit. It felt like running into a brick wall. Pencilmate's thumb fell limply to the side of his hand. As Russel bore down once again, Pencilmate flipped his floppy thumb to the side, shaking off the cobwebs—desperate for some way to gain an advantage.

Russel drove his thumb downward once again toward Pencilmate's. Suddenly, desperately, Pencilmate's thumb pulled a tiny metal folding chair out from thin air, swinging it at Russel's thumb.

WHACK!

The tiny chair collided with Russel's knuckle. The champion dropped his pained thumb down. Pencilmate felt his thumb wearily cover Russel's.

"One . . . ," the referee called out.

"Two . . ." Pencilmate pressed down harder on Russel's thumb.

"Three!" the referee finished his count as the crowd erupted. Pencilmate had not only won the tournament and scored points to pad his lead in the Pencilympics, but he beat the thumb-wrestling world champion!

A ring attendant yanked the world championship belt from around Russel's waist and placed it on Pencilmate's shoulder. Pencilmate looked over the crowd in awe. Was this his life?!

Later, following the match, Pencilmate was walking home and admiring his new championship belt when Russel appeared, seemingly from out of nowhere, in front of him.

Russel glared at the new champion as he pulled back a fist, ready to strike. Pencilmate cowered in front of the former champion. Russel threw his hand toward Pencilmate, but instead of hitting him, Russel shook his hand.

"Congratulations!" Russel bellowed happily. He pulled out two bottles of water, handing one to Pencilmate.

"Always remember to hydrate! Cheers!" Russel said, smashing his water bottle into Pencilmate's, sending fountains of water everywhere before hopping in his limo and driving away.

Pencilmate high-fived his muscular thumb once again and prepared for the next contest. He was almost there . . . The quadrillion dollars were soon to be his.

CHAPTER SIX

To prepare for the second-to-last event of the Pencilympics, Pencilmate needed a skateboard, so he went to his local skate shop to buy one. He gazed at the rows and rows of skateboards hanging throughout the shop. There were so many with incredible designs on them. He picked one off the rack that featured a dragon eating the world.

"That looks so cool!" he whispered.

Pencilmate carried his new board to the counter.

"I need to buy this skateboard for the Pencilympics," he told the clerk.

The clerk shook his head. "No, no. That won't do. The skater doesn't choose the board. The board chooses the skater."

Pencilmate's face contorted into a confused expression, which was easily read by the clerk.

"Go back through the boards. Your board will choose you. Trust me," the clerk said.

Skeptical but still in need of the board, Pencilmate returned to the racks of skateboards. There were so many that he thought looked incredible, but every time he picked one up, the clerk would cough and shake his head.

His frustration growing, Pencilmate turned to leave the store. Just then, he felt something tap his ankle. He looked down at his feet and saw a skateboard nudging him. He picked it up and was shocked by the design he saw on the board: a picture of a devilish monster getting sprayed in the face by an open soda bottle. It looked just like the incident with the monster from a few days earlier! That wasn't possible! Was it?

The clerk cleared his throat and said, "That's the one. It picked you!"

Pencilmate shrugged and paid for the board. Outside the skate shop, he jumped on the board and rode it down the street. It felt pretty good, like he and the board were becoming one. It was almost as if the board could read his thoughts!

He rode the board to a nearby skate park to practice for the next day's event. There, he and the board spent hours perfecting his tricks. They flipped, grinded on ledges, and got air.

Pencilmate was amazed at the synchronicity he felt with his board. No wonder the board picked him. They really had become a perfect team. There was no way he would lose tomorrow! With this board, he was unstoppable!

The next morning, Pencilmate arose early. Dressed in his required protective gear—a helmet and knee and elbow pads—he set off on his board for the Pencilympics skateboard course. Confidence oozed from him. After all the events, his score was in a good position to win the whole Pencilympics. If—no, when—he got a solid score today in the skateboarding event, he would be so far ahead, no one would be able to catch him.

Of course, if he failed today, he would fall behind and really have to work hard to win the final event tomorrow, the triathlon. But that wasn't going to be an issue, Pencilmate knew. With his board, he'd be unstoppable.

He stood atop the half-pipe for the event's first round, the nose of his board hanging just over the edge of the half-pipe. With one foot on the board, he pushed off with his other foot. Or at least he tried to.

The board didn't budge. He pushed again. Nothing. No matter how hard Pencilmate pushed with his foot, the board refused to move. It just stood there at the top of the half-pipe.

Feeling frustration rise within himself, Pencilmate kicked the board. It was like kicking bricks! He hopped around on one foot, holding his sore toes. Angrily, he got down close to the board and grabbed it with both hands.

Suddenly, the board burst to life! It went tearing down the half-pipe at tremendous speed! Pencilmate held on to the board with both hands, trailing behind it like a flag flapping in the wind.

"Ahhhhhhhhhh!!!!" Pencilmate screamed as the board raced down the ramp of the half-pipe and then up the other side. Before he knew it, Pencilmate was airborne. The board carried him skyward like a rocket. Pencilmate felt gravity's pull under him as he soared up. His hands started to slip off the board. He tried regaining his grip, but it was no use. Pencilmate crashed back down onto the half-pipe, sliding slowly face-first into the center. Moments later, his board gently rolled into the pipe and next to him.

He looked up at the scoreboard. He actually lost ten points from his overall score! Glaring at his skateboard, he carried it to the next part of the event, the obstacle course.

Built like a regular skate park with rails and ramps, the obstacle course allowed skaters to show off their best tricks in a competitive environment. Pencilmate knew that if he was going to recover from the disaster on the half-pipe, he would have to wow the judges.

When it came time for his turn in the course, Pencilmate pushed off down the first ramp. No problems this time! He moved down the ramp, picking up speed. He kicked up his board in a flip trick and landed it successfully.

Relieved, Pencilmate jumped his board onto the next obstacle: a rail. Flipping perpendicular to the rail, he felt the board sliding smoothly until it reached the midpoint of the rail, where it suddenly stopped. Pencilmate's momentum from the board carried him through the air once again. He was only stopped when his body slammed into a wall.

Literally peeling himself off the wall, Pencilmate trudged back into the course. Grabbing his board off the rail, he stormed off, defeated. He looked up at the scoreboard one more time and saw that he'd lost another dozen points from his total score. Worse, because of his two epic fails in the event, he was disqualified from competing in the rest of the skateboard competition.

Angrily, he sat down on the bench. Tomorrow's triathlon was now his last chance to win the coveted quadrillion-dollar prize. Devastated at the day's outcome, Pencilmate rested his chin in his hands, watching the other competitors score huge points in the half-pipe and obstacle course.

"Stupid skateboard," Pencilmate grumbled. However, he heard someone laugh in response. He looked around. There was no one sitting near him. Yet the laughter was growing.

Beneath his feet, the skateboard started to move. Pencilmate was awestruck as the board wheeled itself out from under him and stood up on its rear wheels as though it were a puppy standing on its hind legs.

The image of the monster and the soda began to change. Pencilmate's eyes grew wide. He had never seen a picture of something come to life. Within seconds, the image of the monster peeled itself off the board and grew much larger.

Standing in front of Pencilmate was the very monster he'd encountered days earlier.

What is happening?! Pencilmate thought.

The monster grinned a devilish grin. "So, Pencilmate, you thought you could trick me with the soda, did you?"

Pencilmate tried to speak but couldn't open his mouth. The monster drew himself close to Pencilmate's face.

"As you probably figured out, I controlled the skateboard out there! Next time, don't pull a prank on the devil himself!" the monster laughed.

Pencilmate shared an uncomfortable laugh in response.

"You're all right, kid," the monster said. He slapped Pencilmate on the back and walked away.

Pencilmate shook his head in disbelief at the wild day. But he couldn't let the day's events distract him. Tomorrow was the final event. It was his last chance. He *had* to win the triathlon and the Pencilympics prize.

CHAPTER SEVEN

The sun was hot, but Pencilmate didn't care. He'd made it to the final event of the Pencilympics: the triathlon!

This will be a piece of cake, he thought. Swim, bike, and run . . . he was confident in his abilities in all three. The quadrillion-dollar prize was so close he could taste it.

He stood alongside his fellow challengers at the edge of a lake. His scores from the previous events placed him in the middle of the pack, but if he dominated these events, he would jump to first place. Dressed in a wetsuit, Pencilmate stretched his arms and legs.

"Swimmers! On your marks," a judge's voice bellowed through a nearby loudspeaker. Seconds later, a horn blared, and the swimmers all jumped into the lake.

Pencilmate swam furiously. He sensed his competition was passing him in the water. Their kicks and strokes splashed so much water in his face, he was finding it hard to breathe.

This presented Pencilmate with a difficult challenge: The inability to breathe was slowing him down! He faced a devastating loss if he didn't catch up quickly!

Suddenly, he had an idea. He reached down into his wetsuit and pulled out his inhaler. Usually reserved for asthmatic episodes that occasionally beset him, this inhaler would help him through the swimming portion of the competition. He puffed on the inhaler and was able to breathe normally despite the gallons of water that were hitting his face.

He kicked and stroked harder than he ever had before, and soon, he reached the shoreline at the end of the lake. He didn't come in first, but he didn't come in last, either. This bought him enough time to throw off his wetsuit, pocket his inhaler, and jump on a bicycle for the second leg of the event.

Feeling recharged from the swim, Pencilmate pedaled his bike in a whirl. He rapidly caught up to the leading cyclist. The two rivals rode their two-wheeled chariots neck and neck, throwing shady side-eyes at each other. Pencilmate felt his determination inside him grow and powered up his legs. He quickly passed the lead rider, surging way ahead in the race. His confidence growing to the point of cockiness, Pencilmate thought he'd show off his impressive cycling tricks.

He raised his hands above his head, pedaling as fast as ever.

"No hands!" he cheered.

He stood on the bicycle's seat, flexing his muscles and waving to the crowd. For his final trick, he lifted his right foot off the seat, balancing on his left foot. That grand finale lasted for only a couple of seconds as Pencilmate began to wobble. He was losing his balance! Panicked, he reached for the bike's handlebars.

But it was too late! Pencilmate flipped over the front of his bike, causing the bicycle to soar airborne over him before crashing to the ground.

The other cyclists were catching up! Pencilmate raced to his battered bike just as three other competitors approached from behind. He jumped back onto his bike and pedaled with all his might toward the end of the bicycle track. He was neck and neck with a couple of other riders, though not for long, as they all crossed the finish line of the bike portion simultaneously.

Pencilmate quickly made his way to the running track for the final part of the triathlon. He sprinted his way to the head of the pack but felt his energy waning. Exhausted, he fell to the ground.

Pencilmate reached into a pocket of his shorts, pulling out a donut. He quickly inhaled the pastry with other runners laughing at him as they passed. But Pencilmate didn't care. The tasty treat gave him enough energy to leap back to his feet!

With more runners passing him, Pencilmate returned to the race. He was still very tired; his feet felt like cement. Desperate to catch up to the lead runner, he decided to pull out his secret weapon . . .

A bag of Jimbo's Superstrong Instant Coffee and a mug! Mixing the contents of the entire bag in his mug, Pencilmate drank the whole thing in one gulp and threw the mug away. He felt the energy-boosting liquid course through his body.

He started to run. At first it was a jog. Then a sprint. Pencilmate's feet carried him faster than he'd ever moved before! He passed runner after runner as his legs accelerated. His feet felt like they weren't even touching the track anymore. Instead, they were a whirling blur. He rapidly approached the head of the mass of runners when the coffee suddenly wore off!

Crashing to the ground with runners passing him on his right and left, Pencilmate grew desperate.

If he was going to win the quadrillion-dollar prize, he had to dig down deep—into his pockets. He pulled out a Jimbo's Energy Candy Bar he'd saved as a last resort for just such an emergency. He tore the package apart and inhaled the energy bar.

His body jerked. His face contorted. Pencilmate felt his entire being rise from the ground and run. The crowd watched in awe as Pencilmate transformed into what they later would describe as a blue lightning bolt. He flashed past all the other runners in a blink of an eye. The finish line was close, but none of the other runners were.

Pencilmate crossed the finish line, breaking the tape at the end of the line and setting it on fire from his incredible speed! He'd won the triathlon but couldn't stop running! So, he didn't. He raced around the track, again and again and again, passing all the runners with each lap. He crossed the finish line six more times before the runner who came in second had crossed for the first time!

After what felt like hours but was actually only seconds, Pencilmate slowed himself to a stop. A little dizzy and very tired, he caught his breath.

"Our winner of the Pencilympics: Pencilmate!" the judge called through the loudspeaker. The crowd roared their approval.

Pencilmate waved to his adoring fans as he took his place atop the winner's podium. The judge presented him with a large gold trophy. Pencilmate held it high above his head in victory!

"When do I get the quadrillion dollars?" Pencilmate asked the judge.

The judge laughed. "Quadrillion dollars? What are you talking about?"

Confused, Pencilmate furrowed his brow. "The grand prize for the winner . . . When the Pencilympics were announced, they said it was a quadrillion-dollar prize."

The judge laughed again, saying, "No, no, no. It's not a quadrillion dollars! It's a quadrillion doll hairs!"

Pencilmate's mouth gaped open, and he thought back to the initial announcement.

"HEAR YE, HEAR YE! Don't miss your chan<sktch> to compete with the grea<sktch>est athletes in our wor<sktch> in the Pencilympics! Sign-ups begin today here in the p<sktch>! Don't miss your chance to win the quadrillion doll<sktch> prize!"

The static! Pencilmate slapped his forehead. He'd misheard! All that work for nothing!

Behind him, Pencilmate heard a beeping sound. A massive dump truck approached.

Pencilmate looked up at the heavy machinery as it dropped its bed backward, burying Pencilmate beneath a mountain of hay-colored doll hair.

Under a quadrillion strands of synthetic hair, Pencilmate peered out into the crowd, who were still cheering his victory. He may not have won a quadrillion dollars, but he was still the victor of the Pencilympics. And that was pretty sweet—even if he had no idea what he'd do with a mountain of doll hair!